A.R level 3.7

R.L. 3.7

THE GREAT DEWEY HUNT

Toni Buzzeo

Illustrations by
Sachiko Yoshikawa

Janesville, Wisconsin
www.upstartbooks.com

*To all of the learners at Jewett-
Hanson schools in Buxton, Maine.
And especially to Dolores, Mary,
and Laurie.*
—T. B.

To Wayne and Kinu.
—S. Y.

Published by UpstartBooks
401 S. Wright Road
Janesville, WI 53547
1-608-743-8000

Text © 2009 by Toni Buzzeo
Illustrations © 2009 by Sachiko Yoshikawa

Love Your Library

On Monday, Mrs. Skorupski swooped over to greet my class at the library door.

"Hello Hugh Abernathy," she said. "So, you're line leader today?"

She pointed me toward the "Knowledge Nest." The light glinted off her rhinestone earrings. The left one spelled out 000. The right spelled 900.

My twin brother Louis nudged me. "Check out her shoes."

More rhinestone numbers! They were also pinned to her collar, holding her sweater closed, and decorating a ring on each hand. Ten numbers in all.

"What's our librarian up to now?" I whispered.

A squeaky little voice piped up from the picture book section. "Carmen! Carmen!" It was Freida Peña in her detective gear.

My next-door neighbor and classmate, Carmen Rosa Peña, growled at her little sister, "You're such a twerp." Then she sailed by squawking, "Dibs on the top row of the Nest."

Freida looked sadly after Carmen. But Louis waved, and I made rabbit ears over Louis's head. Finally, Freida giggled.

"Okily dokily," Mrs. Skorupski began when our class was seated. "Time to get started!"

Carmen waved her hand wildly and didn't wait to be called on. "It's URGENT."
She fluffed her hair. "I have to perform at the Girl Scout jamboree in TWELVE
DAYS! I need a book of puppet plays right away."

"Let's discuss it later," Mrs. Skorupski said. "Now, who can tell me about Dewey?"

I raised my hand a moment too late. Carmen was already answering Mrs. Skorupski's question. "Even my clueless second grade sister knows about Melvil Dewey, the world famous librarian who invented the Dewey decimal system."

"Hey Mr. Dickinson—decimals," Louis said. "Just like math class."

Our teacher, Mr. Dickinson, winked at him. Everyone knows Louis is captain of the Liberty School Math Team.

Carmen glared. "It's NOT like math class. It's about BOOKS!"

"Actually," Mrs. Skorupski reminded her, "it IS like math class. Remember the decimal point that comes after the first three digits on any nonfiction book? Well today, I'd like you to explore the Dewey numbers in teams of two. I'll pair you alphabetically by last name."

Louis and I pinky-shook. Abernathy was the first name on Mr. Dickinson's class list.

Next, Mrs. Skorupski clicked a list of rules up on the electronic white board. "Any questions?"

☑ Use a shelf marker at the shelves.

☑ Find ten interesting nonfiction books from your team's Dewey range.

☑ Make sure each book has a different subject and a different Dewey number.

☑ Get back to the Nest in fifteen minutes with ten books.

Carmen raised her hand. "Is there a prize?"

"Absolutely," Mrs. Skorupski said. "Each team that completes the job gets a highly sought-after Dewey decimal system bookmark."

"Oh." Carmen sighed. "I hope there's a GRAND prize."

Strange and
Mysterious
Underwater Creatures

By L. Ness

Mrs. Skorupski assigned us the 000 category, and we were the first team back with our ten books.

"Write the full Dewey number from the spine of each book on a sticky note in the lower right hand corner of the front cover," Mrs. Skorupski said.

When all teams were finished, Mrs. Skorupski turned to Louis. "In one sentence, please summarize the kinds of books in the zero hundreds section."

"We found a little bit of everything," Louis said. "Encyclopedias, almanacs, books on the Internet, and books about strange creatures that might be real."

"Exactly," Mrs. Skorupski said. "That's why we call your section GENERAL KNOWLEDGE." She turned the document camera on. "Hugh, why don't you share your books with the group?"

When I finished, we carried our "highly sought-after" Dewey bookmarks back to our seats and listened to the other teams' presentations.

When it was Carmen's turn, she said, "The 800s include famous stories plus jokes, poetry, and plays. But I didn't find a single puppet play book and I REALLY need one. Besides, someone tried to trick us!" She scowled at me. "We found a football book right in the middle of our section."

"A misfiled book!" Mrs. Skorupski exclaimed. "Thank you. Once they're on the wrong shelf, they are almost impossible to find."

At the end of the presentations, Mr. Dickinson said, "Now we'll be checking out all the books you've collected, 000s to 900s, and continuing the project in our classroom."

"Wait!" said Carmen. "What about the GRAND prize?"

For the next two nights, our team homework was to create a list of ten small objects to represent our ten 000 books and then to collect as many of the objects as we could.

"Hey Freida," I said that afternoon as we all got off the bus. "Want to help us brainstorm?"

"Sure! Can I brainstorm AND contribute objects?" Freida asked.

"You can have my sister AND her objects," Carmen grumbled from behind us. "She's NOT helping MY team."

The three of us came up with ten perfect objects. I contributed my small furry Bigfoot, a space alien action figure, and a 3D red plastic question mark. Louis added a tiny computer keychain and a picture postcard of the public library. Plus, he drew a map showing the lost continent of Atlantis. Freida added a rolled newspaper from her dollhouse, an ad for encyclopedias from the recycling basket, a rubber sea monster from the science museum, and a miniature blank book.

Freida gazed at the pile. "It's a prize-winning collection!"

"We couldn't have done it without you," Louis told her.

On the bus Wednesday morning, Carmen was still grumpy. "There's only one book of puppet plays in the whole library, and it's stolen!"

"Or misfiled," I reminded her.

"Stolen," Carmen repeated. "And I need it NOW."

000

100

200

560

600

At school, Mr. Dickinson collected our lists and objects. Mrs. Skorupski promised to gather any missing objects from the lists.

All week, items piled up in the library display case, separated by Dewey category. Everyone wondered what would happen next.

700

300

400

800

900

The following Monday morning, the display case was empty except for a big sign.

I poked Louis. "Hey, Freida is in Mr. Hester's class."

"Uh-oh," Louis muttered. "If only Carmen were absent today."

THE GREAT DEWEY HUNT!

Hosted by Mr. Dickinson's fourth grade for Mr. Hester's second grade.

11:00 a.m. today.

After morning announcements, we returned to the library. Mrs. Skorupski was decked out in Dewey tights and a shawl with dozens of pictures, each with a Dewey number underneath.

"Hurry, reshelve your ten books," Mrs. Skorupski said. "Don't forget! Proper Dewey order—and leave the objects where you find them."

Every time Louis and I shelved a book, we found its matching object on the shelf nearby.

"Hey," I said. "The objects show where the books are filed on the shelf."

"Right-o," said Mrs. Skorupski. "They're for The Great Dewey Hunt!"

At 11:00 a.m. sharp, we squeezed into the Nest next to Mr. Hester's class. Mrs. Skorupski asked Louis to tell the second graders about the Dewey decimal system.

"It's a system for organizing the nonfiction books in the library into ten categories," Louis said. "That way, all of the books on the same topic are shelved close to each other."

"Wow," said Mr. Dickinson. "That earns a 'Homework-free Night' pass, Louis!"

"You can't depend on it, though," Carmen grumbled. "Sometimes, the most important books are MISSING."

Mrs. Skorupski just went on with her instructions. "Second graders, you will form nine two-person teams and one team of one. Each team will have a pair of fourth grade consultants."

Freida spoke right up. "I'll be the team of one."

"Then we'll be Freida's consultants," Louis volunteered.

"Hey, that's not fair," Carmen said. "Then they'll only have ONE second grader."

"But Freida will have twice the work," Mr. Hester said. "Carmen, would YOU rather work with your sister?"

Carmen folded her arms. "NO thanks."

"Good, then, let's begin," he said.

"There are only three rules for The Great Dewey Hunt." Mrs. Skorupski clicked them up on the white board.

RULES FOR THE GREAT DEWEY HUNT

792.8

629.2

636.8

☑ Locate the objects listed on your sheet; then find a matching book on the shelf nearby.

☑ Ask your fourth grade consultants to double check the book; then write its title and Dewey number next to the name of the object.

☑ Look for a better choice if your fourth grade consultants say your book and object don't match.

"Now," said Mrs. Skorupski. "Any questions?"

Carmen's hand shot up. "Is this when we win the GRAND prize?"

Even without a partner, Freida was lightning fast as she zipped from one Dewey category to another.

She snatched up a small Buddha statue and a book on Buddhism in the 200's.

She skipped back to us shaking a snow globe of Cinderella and Prince Charming along with a copy of the fairytale.

I heard another second grader shriek when she spotted the hairy tarantula toy in the 500's, but Freida just set it on her shoulder and grabbed a copy of *Spiders of the Arizona Desert*.

Next, Freida handed me a toy sailboat and a book titled *Into the Wind*.

"Great job," I said. "Sailing is in the 700s, but books on sailboats are in applied science. You got it right!"

It wasn't until she was in the 800s that she slowed down for a minute. She skipped over and handed me *Performing Puppet Plays for Holidays*. "I think it's a good match for the little theater masks, but the number is 791.53!"

"Hey, a misfiled book!" I said. "You know what to do with this one, right?"

Freida giggled and nodded. She tucked the book under her arm and rushed off to find a correct match. Then, she handed Louis *Plays for Young Audiences* instead.

"Almost finished," said Louis.

When Freida found her last object and book, the three of us let out a loud whoop.

"The first team is finished!" Mrs. Skorupski handed us the 000 pennant. "Who'll be next?"

When everyone was done, Freida walked over to Carmen.
We followed behind.

With a big grin, Freida handed Carmen
the missing book.

Carmen screamed and grabbed it.

"Nice detective work, Freida!" I said.

"Yeah, for a *change*," said Carmen.

"Looks like you got your GRAND prize after all, Carmen," said Mrs. Skorupski.

Then Mrs. Skorupski turned to the second grade teams. "Okily dokily, second graders. Line up in Dewey order, face the fourth graders, and hold those flags up high."

The second graders hurried to obey.

"Freida?" Mrs. Skorupski turned to her.

"Ready, set, FLIP!" Freida called, and we all cheered.